Bruno
Springs Up

by
Sylvie Daigneault

HarperCollins*Publishers*Ltd

http://www.harpercollins.com/canada

96 97 98 99 First edition 4 3 2 1

Printed and bound in Hong Kong
Design by DOUG PANTON INC.

Canadian Cataloguing in Publication Data

Daigneault, Sylvie
Bruno springs up

ISBN 0-00-224411-X (bound)
ISBN 0-00-648124-8 (pbk.)

I. Title.

PS8557.A4459B786 1997   jC813'.54   C96-931571-6
PZ7.D34Br 1997

To Céline

With the sweet breeze of spring came the monarch butterflies. They had traveled a long way to reach Bruno's forest. Many of the birds had also gone south to escape the cold winter. Now they were all flying back to join their friends who had stayed in the forest. The trees were filled with birds and butterflies, and the earth below was sprinkled with crocuses.

Bruno had slept soundly throughout the long winter months, but the birds sang so loudly that morning, he suddenly awoke.

Bruno rubbed his eyes vigorously and tumbled sleepily to the door of the cave. Outside, his parents, Gregory and Clementine, were already busy with spring cleaning.

Bruno stretched his body and announced himself with a long and roaring yawn.

"Good morning, Bruno!" Gregory said. "You must be hungry."

"Yes, I'm starving!" said Bruno. "Let's go to the falls and catch our breakfast."

 The water of the falls was running wild and cold. Gregory bathed in the rushing stream, where Bruno could see big fish.

"This one! This one!" Bruno shouted every time a fish swam by, and every time Gregory caught it in his big wide paw.

Bruno, Clementine and Gregory ate one fish after another until their tummies felt round and full.

The cool swim and his big breakfast filled Bruno with energy. "Can I go visit my friends, Leo and Leah?" he asked his parents.

Gregory and Clementine looked a little doubtful.

"It's not far, really," Bruno pleaded. "I know the way—I'll be fine!"

Clementine wanted to visit their neighbours, the raccoons. Gregory wanted to catch up on all the forest news. They knew that Bruno would soon get bored, so they agreed to let him go play with his friends, the twin rabbits.

"Be careful!" Gregory called out as Bruno set off with confidence.

Bruno enjoyed his first run through the forest after being asleep for so long. He soon spotted Leo and Leah's house in the distance, and hurried toward it. But when he got there, the door and the windows were boarded shut and there was no sign of his friends.

"Where can Leo and Leah be?" he wondered. "Why would they leave their home?"

Suddenly, small cracking sounds interrupted Bruno's thoughts. Was that a white tail running behind the bushes? He dashed after it, calling for his friends.

"Leo! Leah!" His voice echoed through the deep forest.

Soon Bruno realized that he had lost his way. He tried to remember which direction he had come from, but he couldn't. He looked up at the sky to guess how long he had been gone.

"Maybe I'll be able to see home if I climb a tree," Bruno thought, scrambling up the biggest tree that he could find.

When Bruno reached the top branches, all he could see were birds' nests and more trees. A little frightened now, he climbed down, wondering what to do next. As he got to the bottom, he could hear a mumbling sound coming his way.

"It must be Joe, the old fox," Bruno said to himself. "He's the only one who mumbles like that!"

Well, Joe might be old, but he still had a good nose. In one quick sniff he knew that Bruno was near.

"Little Bruno!" he called out. "What brings you to this part of the woods?"

"I was looking for Leo and Leah," Bruno explained. "They don't live at their old house anymore. Have you seen them lately?"

"Hmmm. No, I haven't," answered Joe. "Perhaps they went to the farm to gather vegetable seeds. Why don't you take a look for them there?"

Old Joe showed Bruno the way back to the forest trail and waved goodbye to him at the edge of the farmer's field.

Bruno was about to cross the field
when he spotted a big bull grazing
on a nearby hill.

"I must hide somehow," Bruno thought frantically. Grabbing a thick branch, he covered his furry brown back and set out bravely across the field.

When Bruno had almost reached the farm, he dared to peek at the bull again. The fierce red eyes were looking straight at him! In panic, Bruno dropped the branch, scrambled over the farm fence, fled through the chicken yard and ran into the barn. He hid behind the door.

"Whew!" he gasped. "That was a close call!"

"Shh!" whispered familiar voices.
It was Leo and Leah!

"Bruno! What are you doing here?" they asked together.

"I went through the whole forest looking for you," Bruno explained as he gave his friends a great big hug. "What are *you* doing here?"

"Look, Bruno! We have found all kinds of vegetable seeds. The farmer must have left them in the barn."

"But why did you leave your house?" Bruno asked. He was still confused.

The twins laughed. "Come on, we'll show you," they said.

Leo and Leah proudly took Bruno to see their new home, which was much bigger than the old one.

"What a beautiful house!" Bruno exclaimed. "But where is your mother, Sophie?"

Just then, the door opened, and the little bear was in for a big surprise.

Seven small bunnies rushed out!

They climbed all over Bruno, tickling him from head to toe. Sophie stood in the doorway, smiling.

"Now you see why we had to find another home," said Leo and Leah.

There were many newborns that spring, and the whole forest wanted to celebrate. Alexander, the owl, sent out the invitations. Joe and the baby raccoons made pancakes. Edward, the moose, brought maple syrup. Gregory and Clementine baked a cake, while Sophie was kept busy taking care of her little bunnies.

At sunset, the birds had finished decorating their nests. It was a beautiful spring night. Everyone ate, danced and laughed until the moon showed up.

Soon Bruno realized that Leo and Leah had left the party. He found them sleeping, curled up under a tree. The seven bunnies were nearby, and Bruno couldn't resist tucking his new little friends into their big wicker basket.

The pink stars shining above him made Bruno think of summer. "They are like raspberries in the sky," he thought. Bruno began to dream of eating honey, blueberries and blackberry pies. "Or maybe," he thought, "I'll spend the summer chasing butterflies…"